Little Suzy's Talent Garden

ISHMAEL

Phoenix

Studywell School was unusual. It was one of the few schools in Glorieland where they allowed Miseries to come along and join in the lessons. Although the teachers wanted them to learn about reading and writing and maths, they also hoped the Miseries would learn about Father God and his love for them.

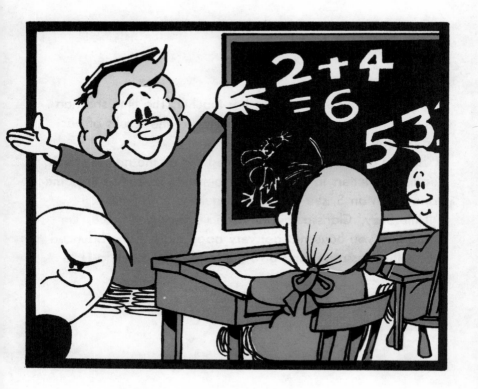

Little Suzy Glorie sat facing her teacher. The time she had dreaded had come: she was going to get the results of her end-of-term test.

Clarissa Glorie, her teacher, called out all the names which began with letters in the alphabet before Suzy's. As her name started with an S, she had to wait quite a long time.

'Little Suzy,' Clarissa said at last, in a very kind voice, 'I'm afraid that you have not got very good marks.' She bounced across the classroom and give the test papers back to Little Suzy.

Little Suzy looked at the low number at the top of the page and saw that she hadn't done very well at all.

'Never mind,' said Clarissa kindly, 'I know you tried your hardest and did your best, and that's what counts.'

Naughty Bob and Eric Miserie were sitting right behind Little Suzy. They peered over her shoulder at her low score.

'Is that all you got?' sneered Bob. 'You must be bottom of the class.' Eric joined in: 'You really are a simple Little Suzy, aren't you?' And both of them burst into laughter.

Poor Little Suzy. She felt the tears welling up in her eyes. It was bad enough to do badly, without having two nasty Miseries telling her that she was useless.

As she bounced slowly home by herself, still feeling very sad, she talked to Father God and asked why he didn't make her clever. Why wasn't she good at anything? Although Father God told her that she was very special to him, she felt so sorry for herself that she didn't hear what he had to say.

Little Suzy turned the corner into Specialgift Gardens, where she lived. There, pinned to a tree, she saw a poster. She bounced over to it inquisitively, as she was sure that it had not been there that morning when she had gone to school.

This is what it said in great big letters.

This Saturday ... Grand Glorie Talent Show ... 6.30 pm in the Hallelujah Hall. A Golden Glorie Award will be presented to the Glorie with the most surprising hidden talent.

Little Suzy felt even sadder as she slouched away. 'I wonder why you have to be clever to be talented in this world,' she thought.

Just then, Suzy heard some familiar chuckles coming from behind the tree with the poster on, and turning round she saw Bob and Eric.

'Why don't you enter, Little Suzy?' shouted Bob, 'and give us all a laugh!'

'Don't be silly!' shrieked Eric. 'She's so stupid she doesn't know what you're talking about. She probably can't even read the poster.'

Once again both of them burst into fits of laughter, and once again Little Suzy felt warm tears running down her cheeks as she bobbed and sobbed her way back towards her house.

That night as Suzy sat on her bed she thought about the talent show. She felt that, even though Bob and Eric were cruel, they were also right. She was useless. She didn't have any talent.

As she sat thinking, she suddenly saw a parcel, wrapped in pretty paper with flowers on it, resting on the table by her bed. It seemed to have appeared from nowhere. She looked at it and picked it up: it was quite heavy.

On it was a large label with the words 'To Little Suzy' written in beautiful handwriting that she didn't recognise.

Quickly, but carefully, Little Suzy unwrapped the parcel, not wanting to damage the pretty wrapping paper. There inside was a brand new cassette player, with a cassette called *Gloriesongs* all ready to play. She knew how it worked because they had one at school, so she put it back on the table and pressed the play button.

The music began. It played a song that she had never heard before, all about how good Father God is. It was the most beautiful melody that she had ever heard.

No one told her what to do next, but immediately Little Suzy was bouncing around the room, dancing for joy.

Later, Little Suzy wondered who had given the present to her. First of all she asked her parents, but they said no.

Then she asked all her relations, and they said no.

Then she asked all her friends, and they too said no.

It was a mystery.

For the rest of that week, every night when she got home, Little Suzy rushed up to her room, closed the door and played the cassette. She just couldn't stop herself dancing to it.

Soon it was Saturday, and time for the talent show. Little Suzy still believed she didn't have any talents, but she thought she would go along anyway to enjoy watching Glories who *were* talented. So, picking up her treasured cassette player, she bounced on down.

Hallelujah Hall was packed with Glories.

Bob and Eric Miserie tried to get in, but when they said that their talent was telling rude jokes, Grandpa Glorie politely told them that they'd do better to take their talent back to the Miseries as the Glories wouldn't laugh at them.

Little Suzy sat on the front row and watched the talented Glories. There were acrobatic Glories, Glories playing musical instruments, Glories with wonderful voices, Glories with clever inventions, Glories who read stories, Glories who wrote poems and Glories who drew pictures.

And that was to name but a few.

After the last performance Grandpa Glorie appeared on the stage and said that everyone was so good it would be very hard to choose the Glorie with the most surprising hidden talent. He would need a little more time to think it through. Then he asked for some music to be played while he did this.

Little Suzy bounced up onto the stage shouting, 'Grandpa Glorie, I've been given a new Gloriesongs cassette. Shall I play that?' Grandpa Glorie told Little Suzy that that would be very nice, and then sat down at the side of the stage to choose the winner.

Little Suzy pressed the play button on her cassette, and turned to sit down again. But as the music started playing, Little Suzy started to dance.

All the Glories stared. Their mouths dropped open in amazement. Even Grandpa Glorie stopped looking at his list of names, and gazed at Little Suzy.

'We never knew that Little Suzy was a talented dancer,' they whispered. 'And that music—where did she get that beautiful music?'

When the cassette had finished, all the Glories bounced on their springs applauding and cheering. Even all the other Glories who had entered the contest clapped. They had never seen anything so good. Grandpa Glorie bounced across the stage and without hesitation handed Little Suzy the Golden Glorie Award.

As the noise died down Grandpa Glorie spoke: 'I never knew Little Suzy was so talented.' Little Suzy blushed, and as she did so Father God whispered, 'I'm glad you enjoyed the gift I gave you. Perhaps now you'll believe that I have given every Glorie very special talents—and that includes you.'

Monday arrived, but Little Suzy decided not to take her Golden Glorie Award to school to show off to her friends. After all, it really belonged to Father God, not her.

Back in the school playground, there were Bob and Eric Miserie. (Now remember—they didn't know what had happened.) Bob reminded Little Suzy that she was simple and stupid, while Eric told her she was useless. Then, as before, they both burst out laughing. But they very soon stopped when Little Suzy started laughing too!

All the other Glories in the playground told the Miseries how stupid they must be if they really believed the best dancer in the school was useless.

Bob and Eric didn't understand, but they could see there was no point in arguing.

Little Suzy whispered a big thank you to Father God.